Not Forgotten

Also by Margaret Bolton and published by Ginninderra Press
Not Another Nun Story
Mother & Son
Tales from Port Vic
Start With a Coffee (Pocket Poets)
Prisoners of War (Pocket People)

Margaret Bolton

Not Forgotten

Not Forgotten
ISBN 978 1 76041 265 4
Copyright © text Margaret Bolton 2016
Cover: main photo – John Warwick Brooke [Public domain], via
Wikimedia Commons; inset – Poppy flower on a green stem © baobabay

First published 2016 by
GINNINDERRA PRESS
PO Box 3461 Port Adelaide 5015
www.ginninderrapress.com.au

Prologue

July 2001

The Hubble family were enjoying their Sunday roast of pork with crispy crackling and baked apples. It was always April Rose who cooked Sunday's dinner. At other times she left the cooking to her daughter-in-law, Sandra. She reckoned that, at eighty-four, she'd done her share of cooking for one lifetime.

April's grandchildren were telling of their week at school, another Sunday dinner tradition in the family.

'Our fantastic soccer team is now at the top of the table,' boasted Tim. For six of his ten years he had lived and breathed footy games of any code, especially if the Bombers were on the field. 'And guess who's leading our team goal-kicking competition? Mighty me!' He flung his arms triumphantly into the air.

'Well, aren't you just the greatest?' retorted Stephanie, the eldest. 'Pity you weren't top of your maths class too.'

'That's enough, Steph,' said her father, Robert. 'It's good to have a diversity of talents in the family. A great scholar, a great sportsman and a great musician.' He winked at Andrea, who sat in the middle, both at the table and in chronological order of the three children.

'I seem to have spent the whole week practising, practising, practising for the end-of-term concert,' lamented Andrea. 'I'm playing "Eine Kleine Nachtmusik" and I still haven't got it right.'

'Oh well, miracles can happen in a couple of weeks,' responded her father.

'Oh, by the way, Grandma,' interrupted Stephanie, 'we have to do a major assignment on World War I. We have to find and research a particular soldier. Mrs Hamble showed us how to find service records for soldiers on the web. But I'd rather do someone we know than some anonymous guy. Didn't your father go to that war?'

'He did indeed, but unfortunately he was killed in France. I didn't ever meet him – I was born after he left and he never came back.' A tear welled in her eye but was quickly brushed away. 'I think I have some stuff somewhere in my trunk that I could show you, some photos and medals. I haven't looked at them for years. I've hung on to them in his memory. You never know what else might be in there. I hope the silverfish haven't got to them.'

'What on earth are silverfish?' Tim asked. 'Never heard of them before. How can fish live in a trunk? What do they do for water to swim in?' He laughed at his own wisecrack.

'They're little insect-like creatures that gobble up anything old and precious, like paper and material,' answered his mother, 'but probably not medals.'

'I'll have a look straight after dinner,' said April Rose, 'while you three are washing the dishes.' She smiled at her grandchildren, knowing how they hated their weekly job and always managed to argue ad infinitum while doing it.

A little later on, April Rose spread out her treasures on the now-cleared dining room table. Robert and Sandra joined Stephanie but the other two were nowhere to be seen.

'This was his identity disc.' April Rose unfolded a small parcel wrapped in tissue. 'Soldiers wore two of them. As their name suggests, they told the world who they were. A green one was still around their neck if and when they were buried, and the red one was eventually sent home to his family. In a way, they were proof that a particular person had died. Apparently the soldiers called them "dead meat tickets".'

'Ugh, revolting,' Stephanie responded.

'And these are his war medals.' She slowly opened a small plush box revealing two medals each attached to a ribbon. 'This one is the Victory Medal. See, it has a winged woman on one side. She is Victory. And on the other side it has the words "The Great War for Civilisation" surrounded by a laurel wreath – a victor's wreath like at the Olympic games.'

'I like the pretty colours on the ribbon.' Stephanie picked it up to admire it. 'It's like two rainbows joined in mirror image.'

'This one is the British War Medal,' April Rose picked up the other medal, 'with St George on horseback trampling the eagle shield of the enemy beneath its feet, and a skull and crossbones, symbols of death. And here at the top is the risen sun of victory. The years 1914–1918 are marked on the edge of the medal.'

'It has a plainer ribbon,' noticed Stephanie, 'just a wide orange stripe with narrower stripes of white, black and blue on the outside. Did everyone get medals like these?'

'Indeed, whether they came home or not. You see them being worn at the Anzac march each year,' intervened Robert.

Looking into the trunk to see what further things might be forthcoming, Stephanie noticed a brown cardboard envelope. She picked it up and carefully opened it. 'What's this huge medallion?' she asked. 'I suppose it's extra special because it's so big! It's got a woman holding some branches and a lion stalking across it. What's that all about? I can see Great-grandpa's name engraved there again, and the words, "He died for freedom and honour". And there's nothing at all on the back.'

'They call it a widow's penny. It was only awarded for those who were killed in action. I'm not sure what all the symbols mean. You can probably find it on the internet,' April Rose explained. 'And did you notice the two little dolphins at the top?' She continued, 'This message of condolence came with it.'

'Let me see,' Stephanie exclaimed. '"He died for freedom and honour",' she read. 'There it is again, those same words: "I join with my grateful people in sending you this memorial of a brave life given for others in the Great War." And look,' she said excitedly, 'it has Buckingham Palace written across the top, so it really did come from the king, eh, Grandma?'

'The king also sent a memorial scroll. This is my favourite memento,' said April Rose as she gently untied and unrolled a large scroll of yellowed paper. 'This was sent to Mother by King George V after Father died. It has the royal coat of arms at the top, and you, Stephanie, can read the message.'

In a solemn voice, Stephanie read it to her parents. '"He whom this scroll commemorates was numbered amongst those who, at the call of King and Country, left all that was dear to them, endured hardness, faced danger, and finally passed out of the sight of men by the path of duty and self-sacrifice, giving up their own lives that others might live in freedom. Let those who come after see to it that his name be not forgotten." And there on the bottom,' she added, 'is his name: Arthur Michael McKayson. Is that really what he was called? I just knew he was Mick.'

'That was his full and official name, but he was always known as Mick Mack,' explained April Rose. She poked about the trunk further and came out with a souvenir bookmark that her father had sent to her mother. 'This was a 1918 job.'

The date on the bookmark confirmed her remark.

'Mother especially liked the embroidered red poppies entwined beneath Australian and French flags. But she didn't realise their symbolism when it first arrived.'

'The silk work is exquisite and so vivid,' marvelled Sandra.

'Do you have any photographs of him when he went to the war?' Stephanie asked.

'Hm, just four,' replied April. 'One before he left, all spick and span in his new uniform, one of me as a baby and one taken somewhere in France with a family. And then there's one of a girl. I wonder what Mother made of this one.'

'Nice-looking girl, but a sloppy-looking kid in the French one,' commented Stephanie. 'Who do you reckon they were?'

'Mother never kept Father's letters, but she said soldiers often visited villages in their time off, and sometimes stayed in people's houses, or more likely in their barns. Perhaps it's one of them. I'm not sure how much significance the French ones hold. They found them in his top pocket when he died, along with the baby photo of me with Mother.'

'You don't think he fancied someone over there, do you?'

'Unthinkable!' April Rose was adamant. 'He would never have done anything like that. He loved Mother, and me too, his unseen one, with a passion.'

'A little bit of passion can go a long way,' was Stephanie's rejoinder.

Her mother intervened. 'Cut the nonsense, Steph. Just because you're a romantic at heart doesn't mean you can attribute that to all and sundry.'

'Okay. Sorry, Grandma. Do you know where your father fought over there? I've read about heaps of battles all up and down the front line from the coast to Switzerland. Which parts was he in?'

'All his letters were headed "Somewhere in France" so that's all I know – that he was somewhere in France. However, he died near a place called Monument Wood, and was firstly buried near the Wood and later transferred to the war memorial cemetery at Blangy-Tronville. Both of those places are not far from Villers-Bretonneux.'

Robert added, 'Villers-Bretonneux has the main memorial to the Australians in France. It's east of Paris. It's a town that holds the Anzacs to its heart. "*N'oublions jamais l'Australie*" – their motto is "Never forget the Australians".'

April Rose got up to stretch her aching knees and make a cuppa, while Stephanie went off to check the internet for the symbolism of the widow's medal.

She was back in only a few minutes. 'The woman is Britannia, the branches are oak, the lion is the empire, the two little dolphins represent the British sea power, and the eagle being torn to pieces by another lion is Germany. I hadn't even noticed the eagle before. Gruesome, eh?'

'Any war is unspeakably gruesome, my dear,' answered April Rose.

Robert stirred two spoons of sugar into his coffee, and lifted the cup for his customary lingering smell of the aromatic coffee. 'The French make good coffee,' he announced. 'Perhaps we could take a trip there to try it, freshly ground and piping hot. There's nothing like it, they say.'

'Could we really? Do you mean it? You're not joking, are you?' Stephanie was excited. 'It would be an awesome trip. And while we're there we could check out that Blangy place where Great-grandpa's buried. And let's not forget the Moulin Rouge. I've always wanted to go there ever since seeing that great film with the dancing dwarves in it. Isn't Ewan McGregor just the hottest?'

'Nicole Kidman ain't half bad either,' quipped Robert, smiling at Sandra. 'Let's go in the next school holidays.'

1

September 1915

Even before he knocked at the door, Jane McKayson knew. She knew at the very moment that she looked up from kneading the bread and saw her young and pimply-faced parish priest striding up the front path and onto the wide veranda, with a pink envelope in his hand, that the news was not good. She could hardly bear to respond to his urgent knocking on the wooden door with its peeling green paint.

She brushed the flour from her apron, wiped away her welling tears and tentatively opened the door. 'Good morning, Father.' Her voice faltered.

'I'm afraid I'm the bearer of bad news. You'd best sit down.' There was no beating around the bush by the young priest. He had had to do this several times before and had found that a direct approach was best. 'I have a telegram from the military. It's about Joe.'

'Noooooo…' Jane wailed, burying her face in her hands. 'Not Joe, my firstborn, my beautiful son.' She fished an embroidered handkerchief out of her apron pocket and blew noisily into it.

Father Dolan put his hand on her arm and waited for the outburst to settle.

Eventually, Jane wiped her tears and looked at Father Dolan with desolate eyes like a lost dog. 'There must be a mistake,' she said. 'Here, let me see the telegram… We had a letter from him yesterday and he was fine then. He's only been at Gallipoli for five months.' Her heart, like a lump of stone, was still banging loudly against her chest.

Father Dolan read the telegram to her. '"We regret to inform you that your son Private P.J. McKayson was killed in action on the night of the 14th instant." That was three days ago, on the feast of the Holy Cross,' he continued. 'What better day to die than in the sure knowledge of the redemptive power of our dear Lord's cross. Joe will be at peace now. And look, it says here that death was instantaneous and without any suffering. That's something to be grateful for, Mrs McKayson.'

Hardly able to speak through her renewed sobbing, Jane mumbled, 'How could it have happened?'

'The answer to that is in the telegram too,' the young priest continued. 'It says, "His battalion was taking part in an attack when a shell fell on your son killing him and wounding a comrade. It was impossible to get his remains away and he lies in a soldier's grave where he fell." We'll remember him at Mass on Sunday and pray for his soul.'

'I'm not sure I could go to Mass on Sunday,' whispered Jane. 'By then, everyone will know of my grief. How can I face them all?'

'Joe is worthy of the honour and glory of a fallen soldier, and I know you will find some consolation in remembering this. And of course there are other women in the congregation who will share your sorrow in a special way.'

'I s'pose so,' conceded Jane. 'At least I've still got Mick.'

The young priest got up and embraced Jane, patting her gently on the back. 'Now I'll go down to the milking shed and break the news to John for you. He'll take it hard too, I guess. God bless you, Mrs McKayson.'

As he made his way down the back to the smelly cowshed past the drooping pepper tree with its pink-paper-covered berries and a few straggly chooks pecking around below it, a kookaburra cackled loud and long.

2

Mick took his brother's death hard. 'It could have been me, but they turned me down, told me I was too skinny.' Only a little younger, he had enlisted for the war in 1915 at the same time as Joe. 'Too thin with a chest measurement of thirty-three inches. What was wrong with them?' brooded Mick. 'I was young and fit and willing.' Still, in his heart, he was glad to have failed, for the thought of killing someone was intolerable to him.

From the time when as a little tacker Mick had been dared by Joe to break one of the duck eggs in a nest in the woodpile, he couldn't bear to kill anything, let alone another person. He had seen that the tiny naked duckling with an eye nearly as big as its head wouldn't live at all. It wasn't as if he didn't see the necessity of war, especially against the Germans, it was just the shooting of another human being that he couldn't contemplate.

Mick remembered confessing the death of the duckling when he made his first confession at St Joseph's, the little dark-stoned church at Tallarook, and scoring three Hail Marys for his sin. How could three Hail Marys possibly make up for a life lost, a murder, even if it was only a duckling?

He also remembered playing Cowboys and Indians in the long dry grass at primary school and being hit in the shoulder by a bow and arrow made of sticks and string. It hurt a lot, but he couldn't cry about it; that would have brought on even worse recriminations. It was all-out war. The other boys were setting out to 'kill' him.

He remembered, too, their time in the military cadets, marching their horses in parade up on the Tallarook oval, he playing his cornet, the band providing the beat for the marchers. At least with a cornet in hand there was no need to carry a make-out gun. He pictured with horror the sabre attached to the barrel of a rifle and the damage that could do to a person.

The two brothers had begun their schooling at the small parish school of St Joseph's, high on the hill in their home town of Tallarook. Then Joe had started high school at Sacred Heart College down on the flat at Seymour the year before Mick did, so when Mick began there he felt at home. They caught the train down the hill on Sunday evenings and back home again on Friday evenings, and stayed with Granny McKayson in Seymour itself, only five minutes' walk from the school. While Joe studied science, maths, Latin and geography, Mick preferred English, French, history and music. Joe enjoyed getting rid of his frustrations in the aggression of footy tackles while Mick excelled at the more tactical art of cricket.

On leaving school, Joe stayed at home to help his father on the farm, getting his hands dirty shearing the sheep, milking the cows and harvesting hay for the horses, while Mick found employment in the State Bank of Victoria on the banks of the Goulburn River at Seymour, enjoying handling lots of money that wasn't his. No dirt for him.

Mick rode his bike the seven miles down the winding road through the bush from Tallarook to Seymour each day. Staying with Granny had lost its appeal as he grew older. The forty-minute ride provided thinking time, time when he was dreaming of good-looking girls and a domesticity of his own. 'It really is time I found someone special,' he thought. It was a different story coming home up the hill. 'First I have to actually meet a girl.' He panted with the exertion of pedalling, sweat running down his forehead. 'How do I do that when I'm shy?'

He had his eye on Maggie Foster. Those clear and brilliant hazel eyes with irises ringed by dark circles seemed to see right through to his innermost being. Her one dimple winked at him when she smiled. How he longed to run his hands through her wavy bob and caress her smooth cheeks. To kiss those lips would be sublime.

'Tomorrow I will make it my business to say hello to Maggie Foster. I'll just have to summon up the courage and do it.'

It was only a few months later that they announced their engagement.

3

Early July 1916

For more than a year, news of battles filtered through to those at home. Long months of stories of heroics and disasters.

Mick was thinking about the war again. Almost daily, names of Australians were listed in the paper – those who had been killed or were missing in action in France. Most of the young men from the Seymour district had already gone off to the war in their khaki uniforms and slouch hats adorned with the emblem of the rising sun. Everywhere, people were talking about those who were still at home, whom they called shirkers. As they had intended, Mick overheard them in the shops and on the streets. Last Sunday, even Father Dolan had preached strongly about the necessity of war. Didn't he know what the fifth commandment was about?

That morning, an old crone had handed her bank book with a white feather inside it over the counter to Mick. It was the final straw. Upset and teary, Mick had left his boss to deal with her invective while he took a break for a hurried cigarette to gather his thoughts.

Ever since Joe had been killed at Gallipoli, Mick had had the niggling feeling that he should take his place. He knew that his parents would be horrified to know that he was thinking like this, so he hadn't discussed it with them. He had, however, mentioned it once or twice to Maggie, his new wife.

Each time, she'd responded with an angry tirade and slamming of doors as she stomped out onto the veranda. 'That's right. Just ignore my feelings about it all!'

On his way home from work, he'd had to skirt around a crowd

gathered on the pavement in front of the railway station to hear an officer from the Seymour military camp trying to recruit the few young men who had stopped to listen. Among the enthusiastic cheering and clapping of locals, some half-hearted boos could be heard. Even older men were beginning to think that they could go.

Mick was not entirely deaf to the recruiting pleas. But he felt a loyalty to the bank now that all the other tellers had joined up. They'd even had to employ a female teller to fill the gap, an unheard-of solution to the problem.

For Mick, it always came down to the conflict between his head, what he knew he should do, and his heart, what he really wanted to do. He would be damned if he went and damned if he stayed home.

Mick and Maggie lived in Seymour now but never missed riding their bikes back up the hill to Tallarook for a Sunday roast with his parents. Jane would not allow any talk of war at the table. The memory of losing Joe was still raw.

Back at home that night, Mick brought the subject up again. 'They're so desperate for men that they've dropped the height and chest measurement requirements for enlistment,' he said to Maggie. 'I reckon I could get in now if I made up my mind to go. By the way, this shepherd's pie is pretty good, my wonderful little cookie,' he added, hoping to get her on side.

'What would you be wanting to do that for?' shouted Maggie in reply, pushing her chair away forcibly. She approached her husband, fists raised ready to pummel his chest. 'Why would you be wanting to go and leave me all alone? And what about this baby that we're bringing into the world?' She turned away from him so that he couldn't see her tears.

Mick got up from the table and took her into his arms. 'Just simmer down and listen for once,' he said, trying to stay on an even keel. But she pushed him away roughly.

'What happened to the "I couldn't kill anybody" plea?' Her voice rose to a crescendo. 'What if you get yourself killed, then where would

I be? Up the creek without a paddle, I reckon.' She was more worried about how she would be affected if he went away.

'Let's be realistic about all this,' was his reply. 'You're not the only fish in this great big pond. You know that I don't oppose the whole idea of war. In some circumstances, I reckon it's necessary.'

He waited for Maggie to calm down a bit, then made her a cup of tea before continuing. 'I've been thinking, my dear Maggie, that there must be lots of jobs at the front that don't entail handling a gun or a grenade at all. Perhaps I could go for one of them. Baker, tunneller, grave digger, horse handler – I'd be good at that. Had plenty of experience at home on the farm. Signaller or messenger on a bike – I have years of proof that I'm fast on the bike. Cook or orderly in a hospital – I suppose the hospital would be in tents rather than buildings.'

'You'd still have nearly as much chance of getting bombed as the fighting soldiers.' Maggie wasn't going to concede even one point.

'Yesterday my friend, Ted, told me that his mate was going as a stretcher bearer. There'd be no free hands for a gun there, but it would be dangerous amongst it all with no protection. I'm not frightened of getting hurt. It's just killing someone else that I object to. But Ted's got a point. It's a job with a bit of honour and glory that would make it worth going over there. I'll check it out.'

'You do that,' snapped Maggie. 'Don't worry about me at all.'

Maggie wasn't usually this vitriolic. In fact, one of the things Mick loved about her was her easy-going and good-humoured nature. It was just talk of war that riled her.

It was only a couple of weeks later that Mick queued at the enlistment office. He filled out his personal details on the attestation paper, details that would identify him, like age and weight, hair and eye colour, next of kin – anything that could be useful to the army later on. Then, taking the initiative at the interview, he explained to the officer, 'I want to go as a stretcher bearer. Is that possible?'

'It certainly is,' replied Sergeant Thomas. 'But tell me, why a stretcher bearer?'

'Because I couldn't even think of killing another person, friend or foe. I'm not a coward or anything. I'm willing enough to go to war, just not to kill people.'

'I can't agree with you entirely, but many would. Fair enough.' He stopped for a moment to answer the insistent telephone, then continued, 'Stretcher bearers can be attached to a medical corps or to a field battalion. Do you have any preference?'

'Well, I don't have any first aid experience, I'm as strong as a mallee bull, and I've never been to the doctor in my life. What's the difference?'

'Stretcher bearers attached to medical corps often have to do other jobs after bringing in the injured, like transporting patients to the next stage of aid. And they have to do other menial jobs at aid posts or casualty clearing stations, like clearing out the slops. On the other hand, stretcher bearers attached to field battalions are on the front line all the time. And they often play in the battalion band when not in the field.' He stopped for a breath as his fat red cheeks strained at the effort. 'The connection between the two beats me, but that's how it is.'

'Band? That sounds good. I play the bugle and the cornet in our local band. Reckon I could manage a military band, no trouble at all.'

'Got any other useful tricks up your sleeve?'

'I'm quite at home handling horses. Brought up on a farm, you know.'

'Useful stuff for the army. I'll write that on your record. Now let's see about your general health. Notwithstanding your lack of visits to the doctor, you'll need to be inoculated against typhoid, smallpox and enteric fever. You can have those jabs straight away. Over in that building,' he said, pointing to a wooden structure on his right.

4

Late July 1916

It was a sullen Maggie who kissed her husband goodbye as he set off on his bike for the three miles along the valley of the Goulburn River to the hillside training camp on the outer limits of Seymour.

'I s'pose at least you're nearby,' she conceded, 'I want to be able to see you every now and then. But it might be a long time between cuddles.'

'At least it's not like it was with Joe,' said Mick. 'He had to go to Melbourne for his training.'

Tall and wiry, with sandy hair and icy blue eyes, and dressed in his new uniform with his slouch hat and oval-shaped arm patch of black over red, he certainly looked the part of a soldier. Very handsome indeed, his wife thought without saying so. She wasn't about to give him a compliment at this time.

'This outfit is itchy and stiff,' complained Mick, 'but I guess I'll get used to it. Hope I can manage this heavy pack on the bike without falling over.'

At the Seymour camp, he was allocated to one of the many conical tents pitched on open and flat areas halfway up the hill. Gum trees of all sizes from saplings to large shady trees surrounded them. Koalas slept perched in tree forks in the day time and made a dreadful din at night when fighting or trying to attract a mate.

Mick soon found that he knew a few of the other blokes in his tent.

'Good to see you, Ted.' He introduced Ted Harris to the others. 'We've been friends since we were at school together.'

Although the same age and taller than Mick, Ted had been a couple of years behind Mick at Sacred Heart, but at a country school boys from every year level knew each other.

'Hi, Perky. Glad you've got your trumpet with you. Does that mean that you've signed up as a stretcher bearer too? We could be playing in the band together again.' Mick liked Les Perkins, whose personality, as well as his music, often echoed his nickname: he liked the staccato bits.

'That'd be good,' replied Perky. 'And who do we have here?' he asked, turning to the stocky youngster who'd just joined them.

'I'm Owen Aloysius O'Leary, but you can ignore the Aloysius bit. Who'd get saddled with a moniker like that?' Owen spoke with the clipped upper-class voice of a grammar school boy from a well-to-do family. 'I've made it at last. Just celebrated my coming to military age last week, and rearing to go. Jolly good show!'

'And g'day to you too, Hasty.'

Barry Hastings had been in Mick's cricket team.

'I see you've had a haircut. No more long hair streaming out from under your cap as you make a century.'

'Can't say I like the new look,' Hasty retorted. 'Regulations, y'know. Can't fight 'em.' Hasty's hair was standing up like an echidna's spikes. 'By the way, I'm in the artillery division, so I probably won't be seeing a lot of you all during the day time.'

The others introduced themselves too. They had come from further afield across north-eastern parts of Victoria.

The new recruits settled into training. With the yelling of officers always in their ears, their days started with a lecture on some aspect of modern warfare and ended with a lecture on another aspect of modern warfare. Otherwise their time was mainly spent in an excess of marching in formation and on longer routes up and down the hills of the camp with accompanying band playing. Along with that, physical exercise drills for them all, target shooting practice at kerosene tins hidden in bushes for the regular soldiers and first aid classes for the would-be stretcher bearers. Mick liked it when he was rostered to play the reveille to wake the men at sunrise, competing with the magpies' early morning warble; or the last post at sunset, when boobook owls added harmony to his bugle call. Night manoeuvres were difficult on windy and moonless nights, and mock daytime battles using sticks as rifles had an air of unreality about them, especially with regard to stretchering off the injured, however good the acting.

They laughed at some of the incidents when back in their tents at night.

Ted told of falling off his horse when it stuck its foot in a rabbit hole. 'My stick bayonet snapped into pieces when I fell. So I picked up another from under a tree, got back in the saddle, and Bob's your uncle.'

Barry described how he'd tried to shove the shell wrong end first into the big gun. 'Lucky it was one of those old shells with a rim around the bottom so it wouldn't go in however hard I tried.'

'Did you hear Owen groaning as he fell off the stretcher.' Perky's end of the stretcher had given way when they tried to lift Owen.

At the other end of the stretcher, Mick suspected that somewhere in that scenario Owen's moaning had morphed from fake to real. He hoped it wasn't a sign of things to come.

Weekend leave started on Saturday afternoons and gave Mick the chance to go home to Maggie, and not miss out on Sunday roast at Tallarook, while other men hit the pubs with great gusto.

In early springtime when the snow melted on the Australian Alps, the River Goulburn would flood, spilling its waters across the lower parts of Seymour. They said the flood of September 1916 was the worst in living memory. At its peak at Mick's old workplace, water came under the door despite sandbagging, ruining all the flooring and furniture.

'Hope they got the cash out of the safe in time,' he said. 'Just imagine trying to dry out soggy quids.'

Mr Russell's corner grocery store flooded; tins of canned goods floating down the street were quickly snaffled by enterprising neighbours.

As the river rose, the army was called upon to help fill sandbags and build levees.

A few weeks later, the huge task of cleaning up began – taking ruined furniture to the dump, scraping the mud off floorboards, and in some cases dismantling buildings that had become unstable.

Mick and Maggie were relieved that their house was on higher ground. Only their garden was inundated. The silt and debris deposited provided well-needed fertiliser for the vegies and flowers.

'Saves me carting chicken poop,' said Maggie.

Mick and Ted were assigned to dismantle the dangerous timber framework, all that was left of the Shinnicks' house. When her family had woken to muddy water beginning to cover their beds, Mrs Shinnick, with her newborn babe in her arms, her husband and three other children had climbed on to the roof to escape the churning torrent. But the roof had collapsed and Mr Shinnick and the children were washed away and drowned. Even the baby that she had clung to tenaciously for so long was swept away. However, by some miracle, she survived.

All too quickly, the three months of training passed, and it was time to go: to go to war, to do their bit for their country. But not before a few days' leave to say goodbye to loved ones. Mick was worried about how Maggie would cope with her pregnancy and how his parents would manage on the farm while he was away.

'Don't worry,' said his father. 'We'll keep an eye on Maggie and we can hire a bloke to help with the farm work.'

It was at this time too that Australia held a second referendum on the issue of conscripting young men for compulsory war service. Along with a narrow majority of Australians who rejected the proposal, John, Jane, Mick and Maggie had all voted a definite No. In the lead-up to voting day, Mick was glad that he had volunteered to help in this fight for his country. He would have been angry and resentful to have been called up and forced to go.

Quite a large number of people gathered on the long platform at the railway station to see off the 37th Battalion's Fourth Reinforcements. Mick's parents were there; Jane had a large handkerchief at the ready; John had his arm around her waist; Maggie looked forlorn but waved with the rest of them. The local band was there to cheer them on, playing 'It's a long way to Tipperary' and the battalion's anthem 'Boys of battle'.

> We'll march, march, march,
> march on to victory.
> We'll fight, fight, fight,
> fight for our liberty.

Mick almost got caught up in the triumph of it all.

Maggie had packed a couple of sandwiches and apples in a brown paper bag that she gave Mick for the journey to Melbourne for embarkation. On the previous night she had presented her husband with a neatly tied parcel which Mick gently unwrapped to find three writing pads, some envelopes and three pencils. 'Just to encourage you to write often,' she had whispered. 'You will do that, won't you?'

'Of course,' replied Mick, 'at every opportunity that I can.'

He had snuggled down beside her for one last lover's goodbye, but she'd turned away from him, still upset by his decision to go.

Once they reached Melbourne, the soldiers marched down Spencer Street from the railway station and on to the docks. What a farewell! Family and friends whistled their goodbyes and threw red, white and blue streamers up at the ship while bands played popular tunes. Mick wished that he had encouraged Maggie and his parents to make the trip to Melbourne, such was the enthusiasm of the onlookers. The soldiers waved and waved until their friends and relatives disappeared over the horizon as they steamed out through the narrow opening of Port Phillip Bay and westward into the deeper waters of the Southern Ocean.

5

It wasn't until three weeks after he sailed that Mick wrote to Maggie. Maggie read that letter six weeks later. Six weeks when she checked the letter box twice a day, hoping for some news. She was beginning to regret her lack of response to Mick's amorous cuddle the night before he left, fearing that she was now the one out of favour.

November 1916
On the high seas

My darling Maggie,

We reached the Cape of Good Hope after three weeks of sailing in rough seas. As you can imagine, I was quite sick. But I wasn't the only one. It was better to be in the open air of the deck, where we did our physical jerks each morning.

And now we are at Cape Town beneath the Table Mountain with its cloth of lacy clouds swirling over its flat top. We weren't given the freedom of the shore. I think they were afraid that we might all get lost in a pub. But yesterday we marched many miles to the Cecil Rhodes monument, probably to be inspired for what lies ahead. There we were treated to a picnic of fine food, so different to ship's rations. And presented with very welcome gifts of fruit and tobacco.

On the way there, black children with bright eyes and fuzzy hair ran alongside us whooping and laughing and sometimes marching to the tune of our band. And on the way back, white people hung over their fences waving their flags at us and cheering us on. Dare I say it, but it's enough to make one feel proud of being part of the AIF.

Well, my dear, I do hope you are standing up to my absence. I think of you often and long to hold you in my arms again. I trust that our baby within you is growing nicely – you must be beginning to show a goodly bump by now. Please show this letter to Mother and Father too and tell them I'll write to them when we get there, wherever there is. Give them my love and best wishes for a good harvest.

Your loving husband,
Mick

The *Port Lincoln* continued to sail northwards up the west coast of Africa and crossed the equator.

'Father Neptune is definitely not visiting in war time. He is busy elsewhere,' came the message from the captain, 'and no activities of his kind will be entered into.'

Routine on the ship was far from boring. Exercise drills continued and lectures on various aspects of battle tactics continued. Spare time was filled with deck games, boxing matches, two-up, letter writing and sharing stories over a quiet cigarette. Some even tried fishing, supplying a fresh addition to the menu. Occasionally, Mick saw flying fish and porpoises diving in and out of the water. Soldiers had got used to the rolling ship and the pitching in stormy waves that seemed to be mountainous in height. Seasickness was a thing of the past. Although it was still very cramped and airless at night, they tried to sleep soundly in their hammocks packed together like sardines in a tin. As the weather got warmer with their passage northwards, some preferred to sleep on the deck despite the risk of tropical downpours.

Lookouts kept watch by day and night for German U-boats, and blackouts were enforced in the dark. No lights, no cigarettes, it took a while for eyes to become used to the dark. An ever present menace, U-boats could creep up quite close to a ship, causing the shrill blast of the ship's alarm to sound. Then the men would rush to put on their lifebuoys and get to their allocated assembly places, some trembling in fear, although they did their best to keep it to themselves. Engines were then revved up to maximum speed.

'T'would be a bit of a waste to be sunk to the bottom of the ocean even before we got wet behind the ears in any fighting,' whispered Owen O'Leary with a bit of a shudder.

'T'would indeed,' agreed the four friends.

As the vessel followed the coast of Sierra Leone, it became obvious that a U-boat was tracking them, and at a fast pace. The *Port Lincoln* hastily picked up knots and headed on a zigzag course to Freetown on the coast. In the absence of a pilot boat to guide them into the port, the *Port Lincoln* rammed full bore into a sandbar in shallow waters and beached herself there. Even at high tide next morning, she was unable to get off. She'd sprung a gaping hole low down on the bow and was leaking profusely.

'This boat ain't going any further for quite some time,' observed Mick.

'This boat might end its days here,' added Hasty as the men struggled to shore carrying their personal gear along with their share of the other cargo. Hasty was called upon to haul limbers mounted with artillery through the shallows to dry sand.

'Nothing like an unexpected holiday in an exotic location, and all for free.' Owen knew all about holidays in exotic locations.

The soldiers and crew enjoyed an enforced stay in Freetown, exploring the colonial buildings that climbed the hillsides, surrounded by encroaching jungle. The stately residence of the British governor and St George's Cathedral were at the top of the list. The beach provided a good laze and the local hotel and eating places enjoyed unexpected custom.

Most couldn't resist the opportunity to write home about days in this African capital.

'How many letters can one man write on any given day? Give me postcards anytime! Much less writing involved,' said Ted, whose writing ability was limited.

It was like a surprise holiday, except that the morning physical jerks and a short afternoon's march in the hot and steamy weather were still on the program.

'Bad bloody luck about that,' complained Owen.

The food produced by colonials made them think of home again. They only tried the local cuisine after they'd talked to a black woman with a bright yellow headscarf who ran a stall in a side street. She gave them a taste of her okra stew. They had been advised to stay away from areas where black people lived as they were considered to be unsafe and unhealthy.

'Good tucker,' said Hasty.

'You reckon?' groaned Owen, who had been fed fancy food at home. 'It's quite disgusting if you ask me,' he said. 'Just look at the state of her cooking pots. Sure to be crawling with germs.'

'Pull your head in,' said Hasty, 'and be grateful for good food.' Hasty had often had to go without food when he was a kid and things were bad.

It was a week before the first of a series of troop ships passed by and picked up as many men as they could squeeze into their already overloaded quarters. Mick found himself on the *Borda*, which had left Sydney at about the same time as the *Port Lincoln* had left Melbourne.

It was another three weeks before all the ships crossed in convoy into the English Channel and steamed past the Eddystone Light, giving the men some clues as to their whereabouts. The men guessed that they were near Plymouth on the south coast of England.

From Plymouth they caught a train northwards, then marched the last four miles (at least Mick and Perky got lots of band practice along the way) to Larkhill on Salisbury Plain, where they found a large military camp awaiting them. The wood and iron huts were precisely laid out like patches in a quilt. They were given blankets and a straw mattress and shown to their quarters. Here they honed their fighting skills under the instruction of men who had already been to the battle fields of France.

The infantry men dug trenches, practised going over the top, learned the advantages and dangers of new and modern weaponry, and marched what seemed to be endless long distances with heavy packs on their backs.

In the meanwhile, Mick and Perky and the other stretcher bearers practised stopping bleeding, bandaging wounds and slinging broken arms. They practised carrying stretchers in twos and fours, and lifting men bigger than themselves onto their shoulder in a fireman's lift.

And they, too, marched what seemed to be endless long distances with heavy packs on their backs.

The artillery men perfected their teamwork in loading and firing howitzers, practised shooting accurately both in range and direction, and also marched what seemed to be endless long distances with heavy packs on their backs. It always seemed to be muddy or dusty here, conditions that didn't help their activities.

Before the hard training set in, the men were given a few days leave to go to London to visit relatives or just be tourists. Mick and his mates caught the steam train to London using their free passes, and spent their time in buses, enjoying the sights: Buckingham Palace, the Houses of Parliament, St Paul's, the Tower of London and Trafalgar Square with its hordes of pigeons.

'History is surely on show here, and it's all so much older than anything we've got back home.' Mick was thrilled to see buildings that he'd encountered in his history lessons at school.

They caught a boat from London Bridge downstream to the meridian line at Greenwich, and then back upstream past well-to-do suburbs and dingy industrial wastes to Windsor Castle. They got lost time and time again, despite Hasty insisting that he knew the way back like a homing pigeon. Relying on his sense of direction mostly didn't go to plan but friendly policemen were always willing to direct them back to the YMCA in the centre of the city.

Sundays were days of rest from training. 'Yippee, a day off!' After church parade, they were free to explore their wider surroundings. Stonehenge with its great circles of stones aligned to the sun and Salisbury Cathedral with its tall spire and graceful cloisters were wondered at, and many small villages visited by Mick and Ted, who were filled with awe at the antiquity of it all.

'Wonder how many human sacrifices went on at Stonehenge,' chirped Ted, who was attracted to the more gruesome aspects of history.

'Probably none, you nincompoop!' laughed Mick. 'But look what I found,' he said bending down to a small stone object lying there.

'It's a fossil, a small spiral-shaped ammonite shell. This is a whole lot older than the Stonehenge rocks. This place must have been a seabed in times past.'

Mick and Hasty were delighted that cricket was popular at Larkhill. Listening to radio broadcasts of Australia winning the Ashes had always been a favourite pastime. They quickly got themselves into a team that played regularly, sporting khaki shorts rather than regulation whites.

The men had a reputation to live up to. The original Third Division (of which Mick and his mates were reinforcements) was regarded as being one of the finest, most disciplined and best equipped Australian forces to go into battle. But the general insisted that they wear their hats with the brims turned down, a cause of much mirth on the part of other divisions.

Three months passed quickly. Then the men found themselves back on a train and then on a ship to France. This was to be the real thing. They landed on Anzac Day in 1917. Mick thought of his brother Joe again, and sent up an angry prayer asking God why the hell he'd allowed the loss of such a vibrant and loving young man. What was the sense of it all? He shuddered at what the real thing could do to a soldier.

6

April 1917

At home in Seymour and surrounding towns, the women were doing their bit for the war effort. At weekly gatherings at St Mary's parish hall in Seymour, wives and mothers and other patriotic women handed in what they had made.

Ever since the problem of trench foot had come to their notice, they had knitted socks, hundreds of them. Trench foot, they understood from articles in the newspapers, was what happened to feet that had spent too long in freezing and soggy conditions and ill-fitting boots. They became soft and spongy and stank to high heaven, and if left untreated could result in amputation. The women reckoned that regular changes of warm woollen socks were the answer, and got out their knitting needles and wool. No more reading books or magazines, every spare minute was taken by the clicking of needles. Those who couldn't manage four needles and complicated instructions for knitting socks opted for scarves, though not in bright colours.

Jane and a very pregnant Maggie went along to these meetings. The women sat round a long wooden table on hard hall chairs with crocheted rugs over their knees against the frosty mornings, and proudly showed what they had to offer. Jeannie Hastings had sent apologies, she wasn't well, she said, but in reality she was embarrassed at not having the wherewithal to contribute anything. Jane had made some vests of newly shorn sheep skins that she hoped would be sent over, while Maggie had baked some fruit cakes.

'These will give them a treat,' she said. 'Better than hard biscuits.' She imagined Mick fading from his already slender fame.

Mrs Slater, the bank manager's wife, who was the president of the group, asked for suggestions of things to be included in Christmas parcels. 'We've got to think ahead,' she said as she clipped some stray silver curls back into her bun, 'for it will probably take a couple of months for parcels to reach our men.'

'Provided that they're not blown up by some German U-boat on the way over,' Hettie Harris muttered, with her hand over her mouth.

'Cigarettes and tobacco would always be welcome, and recent newspapers, especially local ones so they can know what's happening in the district,' said Elsie Perkins.

'My boy is very fond of puddings, biscuits and sweets,' said Olive O'Leary, whose fancy hat was tilted dangerously over one ear. She secretly hoped that her Owen had lost some weight while overseas.

'Condensed milk would travel nicely, and it's a real treat straight out of the tin. Perhaps we should include a can opener to get the lid off,' giggled Maggie, 'and perhaps some tea to put it in,' she added. 'How do you think chocolate would travel?'

'It's winter over there at Christmas time, so maybe it wouldn't melt too much,' answered Jane.

'What about when it passes through the equator on the way there? I reckon we ought to leave that one out,' objected Mrs Slater. 'Anyway, we must get all these things boxed up and sent off to the Brigade Comforts Fund in Melbourne.'

Maggie poured the tea for everyone, being careful not to trip over her dark blue ankle-length skirt. 'Only one sugar, please. Remember that we're on rations,' she commanded.

Maggie was staying at the farmhouse with her in-laws when labour started.

Jane was an experienced midwife. It was distressing to watch Maggie writhing on the bed in pain, but she knew it had to be. She was astonished at the loudness of Maggie's agonising screams that came in waves with each contraction. 'Whoa! Whoa there, girl,' soothed Jane. 'It's not that bad, and it'll all be over soon.'

'I'm not a bloody horse,' snapped Maggie. She was immediately overcome by the thought that she'd just sworn at her mother-in-law.

At last it was time to push. With an almighty yowl from Maggie, like a dog with its leg caught in a rabbit trap, out came the sweetest little six-pound girl with a smattering of dark hair.

'Well done!' exclaimed Jane. 'What a healthy-looking specimen we have here.'

'I wish Mick could be home to hold her,' said Maggie as she put her baby to the breast for the first time. 'I think I'll call her April Rose.'

'That's a pretty name, dear,' said Jane. 'Not very common, but pretty. Yes, that's a good name for a baby born when her father isn't around to help choose a name. John, come and have a look at your granddaughter.'

John did the burping when April Rose stopped for a breath. He muzzled his moustache onto the baby's cheeks. A loud wail ensued.

'She's used to a soft watery environment, not bristly whiskers,' laughed Maggie. 'But I guess she'll have to get used to your hairy face.'

'Next week we'll go down to the photographer in Seymour and get a photo taken that you can send to Mick,' said Jane.

'He'll like that,' Maggie agreed.

Tallarook
April 1917

Dear Mick,

Our baby daughter arrived safely on the 18th of April. She looks a bit like you but has my dark hair. She is bonny and beautiful, and guzzles her milk like a lamb. I've called her April Rose. There is a photo of her with this letter. I wish you could see her and hold her.

That is the good news, but here is the bad. Unfortunately, a week after her birth, your father had a dreadful accident and was killed. He was rounding up sheep in the bottom paddock when a kangaroo hopped out of a bush and put the wind up his horse. The horse (it was Regal) shied and bolted, taking off over the fence just under that great big red gum. Your father crashed full pelt into one of its low-hanging branches and was killed instantly. I'm so sorry to have to be the bearer of this news. Your mother is not coping too well, so I have decided to stay on up here at Tallarook for a while. We'll get through this together.

How is your war going? We read bits and pieces in the paper. There are so many casualties. I hope you are keeping safe. I have sent you a parcel at the same time as this letter with a few comforts from home. Hope you enjoy it.

I love you lots and lots, my darling husband. Come home soon.

Yours sincerely forever,

Maggie

It was late June before Mick received this letter.

7

In April 1917, as spring slid into summer and bright flowers appeared in the hedgerows along narrow English country lanes, the forces embarked to cross the Straits of Dover to Boulogne in France, then caught a train to a camp on the outskirts of Armentières. This was supposed to be a part of the fighting front with not much action, where the soldiers could gently be introduced to the techniques of warfare.

'Quiet, my arse! Call those blasted guns quiet? It'll be hot out there, I can tell you.' Les Perkins was blunt about the situation.

'They call this the nursery sector, as if we were babies in this endeavour. The real thing apparently comes later,' Mick explained.

On the banks of the River Lys and on the periphery of Armentières, the boys were allocated to their billet in an old barn attached to an abandoned red-brick, slate-roofed house. The hay was comfortable to sleep on, but the biting insects and bugs that lived in it and liked to feast on human flesh weren't very welcome. A couple of cows and some squawking chickens shared the barn. The rooster called his own strident reveille as first light crept through the cracks in the wooden barn door.

The first couple of days were spent getting used to the place. The Seymour boys headed straight for the cobblestone square in the centre of the town, noting stark hulks of bombed buildings.

'Bloody hell, this place has copped a fair whacking,' Perky told it how it was.

Years of shelling had reduced much of it to piles of rubble. Most of the villagers had left for safer places to live, but a few people were still there, making a meagre living from the presence of so many soldiers nearby.

Of course, the incoming soldiers were inducted into the popular song about the village.

> Mademoiselle from Armentières,
> *Parlez-vous?*
> Hasn't been kissed in fifty years,
> Inky, pinky, *parlez-vous!*

Mick was delighted at the great range of bawdy variations in words that soldiers came up with. Some even made him blush but it didn't take him long to sort out the tune on his cornet. He did wonder how many of that sort of mademoiselle still operated in Armentières. Probably quite a few.

On the third day, after dark, Mick and Perky were among those selected to go to the front. Hasty had gone with his artillery section to create havoc in the German lines with their firepower. Issued with steel helmets and respirators, their bags were loaded with a couple of meals of bully beef and biscuit in a tin, a water bottle, and a first aid kit of some bandages, safety pins and a small bottle of disinfecting iodine.

Mick and the other stretcher bearers carried in three stretchers each. They understood that if it got really bad, some of the regular troops would be assigned to help carry out the injured. The troops were marched into reserve trenches, waiting to relieve exhausted men after their spell in the front line. They spent a cold night trying to sleep huddled under their thin blankets in little burrows carved into the side of the trench. Like wombats, thought Mick. But he couldn't sleep. His mind was going round and round with thoughts of the task ahead.

Still half asleep and shivering in the cold, the men were woken at four in the morning to the command of 'Stand to.' The infantry soldiers stood with their rifles at the ready. Pre-dawn was a favoured time for the enemy to attack.

As the sky lightened in the east to a heavy cloud cover, 'Stand down' was issued. There was to be no attack today.

Orderlies arrived carrying containers of bacon and bread. While the rest of the men had breakfast, only a few sentries continued to keep watch for movements in the German trenches on the other side of no-man's-land.

'Tucker's pretty good, considering,' said Ted, gobbling up his portion of the loaf of bread.

'Pity the tea's only lukewarm,' complained Owen. 'I like it hot, with lots of sugar.'

'Get used to it,' snapped Fred, one of the more experienced men, 'for that's how it is out here.'

'What comes next?' Mick asked a soldier who looked like he'd been here longer than him.

'For us, sitting around for most of the day, trying not to get too bored. Good time for a bit of kip, if you can manage it. We usually don't go over the top until dark. Do you play cards? Bridge is popular here.'

'Guess it won't hurt me to learn. I'm good with Five Hundred, though,' said Mick. He noticed some men nearby picking lice from one another's backs. He shuddered at the thought of creepy crawlies on his body.

'Ah, gotta big'n!' exclaimed the lice picker.

'What's going on over there?' asked Mick.

'They're just chatting,' explained Ted with a laugh. 'I've already learnt that lice are called chats around here.'

'Don't think you'll be laughing when they visit you,' said Owen.

'Speaking of creatures great and small, reckon I saw a cat creeping around over there.' Ted missed his ginger moggie that compensated for his lack of siblings.

'That wasn't a cat. T'was a rat. Would that there were some cats here to get rid of the buggers,' said Perky.

'It sure was a whopper. As big as a bunny,' Ted replied.

'Tons of them in the trenches. You'd be advised to keep anything that rats could eat off the ground and out of reach,' warned one of the others.

'Might call the pied piper in,' said Perky with a wink.

So the time dragged on. The crashing boom of the big guns was always in the background. Occasional shells landed just in front or just behind their trench.

'You can hear them coming,' said Ted, while Owen visibly flinched.

'Och weel, the scream gie's a warnin',' said Jock, the red-headed Scot, who'd already been here for a month. 'An' hopefully a wee second tae avoid 'em.'

At six o'clock, a meal of nearly cold stew was carried in by two young privates, who slopped a dollop into each tin lid that served as a plate. Grey and gristly, it seemed to be more liquid than substance and tasted downright awful.

'Guess it's better than nothing,' commented Ted, 'but only just.'

'Better to go into battle with a belly full,' retorted Owen. 'Don't you know that an army marches on its stomach?'

Then the troops, each carrying a rifle or a stretcher, prepared to move forward along a zigzag communication trench to the front line. There they waited until dark, attached a bayonet to their rifle and went over the top at the signal for a raid on the German line. Immediately an enemy machine gun opened fire. An acrid stench of smoke and dust filled the air. Some men had barely moved forward more than a few paces into the open ground before they were mown down by a hail of bullets and shells, like rabbits before a crack rifle shooter.

Stretcher bearer parties of four went into action straight away. Mick and Perky were teamed up with Gav and Johnno, two more experienced men. Wherever possible, they bandaged gaping wounds, then carefully rolled their patient onto the stretcher and covered him with a blanket.

The four stretcher bearers wore white armbands in the hope of deterring German snipers from taking a potshot at them. They lifted the stretchers to their shoulders and headed off towards the aid post in the basement of a bombed-out building on the edge of town behind the trenches.

'This standing high makes us more of a target than regular soldiers creeping over the ground.' Underneath his bravado, Mick was scared.

'All the more reason to keep moving as fast as we can,' said Gav.

'Heavy load this. Hard on the shoulders,' said Perky. 'Sorry, old boy, no offence,' he said in an aside to their patient.

'It's better if you make a thick wad from one of your bandages and place it under the shoulder pad of your coat,' explained Johnno.

'Good advice. Thanks.'

All night, the four men returned again and again to pick up the fallen. Mick and Perky became more and more exhausted as the adrenalin rush of the first few cases waned and as a familiarity with suffering set in. They began to slow down and stumbled once or twice.

'God, this is worse than mustering sheep on foot,' muttered Mick.

'Keep your mind on the job!' barked Johnno. 'There's no excuse for slacking on the battlefield. Each soldier, no matter how badly wounded, relies on us for his life. So get on with it.'

'Right-o,' Mick muttered under his breath, while aloud he acknowledged the directive: 'Message received.'

Back in the trenches at last at the end of a long night, Mick and Perky fell asleep, not even feeling the lice that made their home in their hair.

Next morning, they awoke to the news that the German barrage with deadly accuracy had knocked out several artillery positions, one of which was manned by Barry Hastings's team. A shell had hit him in the hip and left a gaping hole. He was taken in a horse-drawn ambulance from the aid post to the clearing station and then, tagged yellow for urgent surgery, by train to the major hospital on the coast at Boulogne.

'This was supposed to be the learning sector,' said Mick bitterly. 'I'd hate to see a full-blown battle, then.'

'It's not always this bad, mate,' said Johnno.

'Mostly much quieter,' agreed Gav.

'Tell that to Hasty. See if it helps him,' retorted Mick.

'Hope he makes it,' said Ted. 'He's got two little kiddies at home.'

Owen didn't take the news of Hasty's dire injuries well at all. 'Could have been me,' he snivelled. 'Not sure that I'd cope with agonising pain.' With his own welfare uppermost on his mind, he had no sympathy for Hasty at all. He spent the rest of the day propped against a trench post just staring into nothingness.

Later in the week, Mick received a letter from home. He stuffed it into his top pocket until he found a quiet moment to read it. 'I should have a son or daughter by now,' he was thinking as he rolled himself a cigarette. But the letter had taken so long to reach him that it was full of old news, not what he was waiting for.

March 1917
Tallarook

My dearly beloved and only son,

I suppose it will be a while until you get this letter. We hope that you are keeping well and out of danger over there in France. We have seen in the paper that many boys from around here have fallen in the fighting. Paddy Quirk from Hilldene and George Rutherford from Seymour have been killed, and Percy Pickering from Avenal is missing. Such a sad waste, especially as they all survived Gallipoli. Their mothers are distraught. I know how they feel.

Was it very cold over there during the winter? Did you have snow? We have sent you some socks in a separate parcel, hoping they will keep your feet warm.

We are all well here. Maggie is blooming with good health, and is already with us pending the arrival of her little one. A month or two to go and you will have a bouncing baby!

We had a good harvest. Father had some help in bringing the hay in. The autumn lambs are very lively. Your horse, Regal, says hello. I give him a pat for you every now and then.

Must go now and cook the tea. Father sends his regards.

Yours sincerely,

Mother

8

Early June 1917

The word passed along the trenches, 'Today we're moving. We're off to the real thing. Pack your bags and be ready to shove off in thirty minutes. We're going to join the rest of the battalion that we came to reinforce.'

Mick noticed that their shadows indicated a northward direction to their marching. He found it difficult to orient himself with the sun in the opposite half of the sky to that at home. He was trying not to think about his fear but rather to notice the countryside through which their route lay. He started to hum 'It's a long way to Tipperary' in order to get his mind off the fighting. Some of the men next to him joined in.

As night descended, the troops tried to get some sleep but were awoken at three o'clock in the morning by an almighty blast that nearly burst their eardrums and set the earth rumbling.

'What the bloody hell was that?' Immediately they were alert.

'Dunno, but whatever it was, it was an almighty bang.'

'Look out to the east. God, it looks like a heap of volcanoes erupting. Cop the fire and the smoke.'

Black clouds soon became invisible as they blotted out the light of the full moon. Coughing and spluttering on the choking smoke and dust, and with the intense smell of explosives confronting them, they hastily readied themselves to move on again. Word spread that a whole series of mines set deep underground in the hills of the Messines Ridge had been detonated, killing thousands of the enemy. What a way to go!

It wasn't long before Mick's battalion was in the midst of intense fighting again. A heavy barrage of artillery fire aimed to smash coils of barbed wire laid in front of the enemy trenches. This was followed by a creeping barrage providing cover while the front line of the infantry advanced across no-man's-land towards enemy trenches.

It wasn't long before the cry of 'Stretcher bearer, over here' was heard.

Mick and Perky headed out across no-man's-land to an injured soldier.

'Schrapnel's got me in the shoulder,' he said, hanging onto his bloody body, 'then a shot did my leg in. Can't walk. Sorry.'

'It's okay. Here, let's bandage your leg where it's losing so much blood.'

The seeping blood had matted his trousers onto his legs. Mick poured some iodine onto the site.

'Bloody hell man, whatcha doin'? Trying to kill a man before he's dead?' shouted the soldier.

'Easy on, it's only a moment of agony to ward off infection. Reckon you might get a Blighty for this lot. Here, have a guzzle before we set off,' Mick said, passing his water bottle. 'Not too much, though, don't want you spilling your guts.'

'Be bloody good to get out of this hellhole,' said the soldier. 'God, it hurts.' He wiped away some tears with his good hand.

Carefully, Mick and Perky rolled him onto the stretcher, and headed back to the aid post. Their efforts to dodge bullets knocked the wounded soldier around; he nearly fell off a couple of times.

'Here comes a shell,' yelled Perky, alerted by its distinctive swish as it approached. 'Quick, into that crater!'

They rolled into a large shell hole.

The soldier's lower half came off the stretcher. 'Give it a go! I'm not a bloody wool bale that you can just pick up again,' he shouted at them.

'Sorry, can't be helped. Just shut up, else you'll get us all killed,' hissed Perky.

They kept their heads low for a while, before setting out again.

'Quick, run while there's a lull in the shooting,' said Mick.

'Bit hard with a load,' rejoined Perky, 'but I get your drift.'

Soon they were beyond the range of the guns, and in a communication trench. It was harder going in the narrow trenches, even if moderately safer. The stretcher kept hitting the sides of the trench walls, bumping the patient around, not to mention Mick and Perky's knuckles hitting the side often. Softly cursing, they made good time to the aid post: sheets of iron or lengths of wood draped over a makeshift timber frame propped up against a sandbag wall in a sunken road.

'Good luck,' said Mick and Perky together, after they had laid their load at the end of a long line of stretchers waiting their turn to be seen by the medic.

They saw a chaplain whispering prayers into the ears of dying men and dabbing unhurt parts of their bodies with oil.

'Reckon he'd do better to give them hot cocoa,' Perky said.

Back again into the thick of it, they weren't even out of the trench when urgently summoned to another injured soldier.

'Over here,' yelled a private. 'Me mate got buried when a bloody great shell hit the trench. We've pulled two of them out, but there's a couple more under this pile of dirt. Grab a shovel and dig!'

'Their lungs must be full of dirt and muck. They're hardly alive. Best take them to the aid post on our back,' said Mick, hoisting a big burly man over his shoulder in a fireman's lift. 'Quicker that way.' And to the soldier, 'Hang on, matey. Won't be long and she'll be right again.'

Perky and Mick started to jog as best they could.

Well into the night, the stretcher bearers continued to collect wounded men. As long as the moon was in the sky, they could find their way well enough. But as soon as it disappeared under cloud cover, it was difficult not to trip over dead bodies or to fall into gaping holes. Intermittent German flares added an occasional moment of brightness to the scene.

'Dunno whether it's better to see where you're going and risk being shot at or to stumble around in the pitch black safely and perhaps lose your way,' said Mick.

The next day, in the early morning while fog still hugged the ground, the Germans fired canisters of chlorine gas towards the Allies' trenches. It was insidious stuff, causing painful streaming eyes and burning lungs. Some quickly got their respirators on, others copped it before they knew what had hit them. Working while wearing respirators was no mean feat. With only small circles to see out of, and uncomfortable in the extreme, the bearers washed and bandaged the men's eyes and led them away from the front. At a safe distance they sat them on the grass.

'What if I can never see again? Will I be blind for life?'

Their pitiful moaning and cursing deeply upset Mick. 'Wait here while we collect some more, then we'll take you all to the aid post,' he said.

Three more trips netted them more than a dozen men.

'Line up and put your left hand on the shoulder of the man in front of you. Follow him and we'll lead you to the aid post.'

Like a crocodile of children walking the street, the men shuffled along behind Mick while Perky brought up the rear, encouraging the stragglers who found the pain intolerable.

On and on during the night, Mick and Perky, cold, wet and exhausted, carried out the injured. Some of them died before they reached the aid post. Some were so badly injured that they knew they wouldn't make it under any circumstances.

'Perhaps it's better to leave them. Take those that have half a chance,' said Perky, weighing up the situation. 'We can at least leave them with a drink and a ciggie and a little bit of comfort.'

They worked their way nearer and nearer to the enemy trenches, where they found soldiers entangled in the barbed wire that paralleled the enemy front line. Without wire cutters, they were powerless to help them.

'Over here, over here,' came a shout. 'We've captured this pillbox but lost a lot in the attempt. There are both Aussie and Fritz casualties here. Leave them with you. That's good, lads. Gotta move on.'

9

August 1917

Six glorious weeks off, away from the trenches and bombardment. Time out to gain some sort of normality before facing the trenches again. The 3rd Division marched for three hours westward to the little town of Bailleul, miles away from the front, but still near enough to hear the muffled roar of the big guns. The road seemed endless but fairly flat as it passed through the countryside.

The end of summer produced fields ripe with swaying crops of oats and corn, reminding Mick of home. He wondered how his family were. 'Hope it's not a case of out of sight, out of mind. Does Maggie think of me at all? Does she talk about me to April Rose? My little daughter with her dark hair, chubby cheeks and a single dimple like her mother. Beautiful and oh, so cute!' He murmured her name over and over in time with his marching: April Rose…

From Bailleul, the troops caught the train to Wizernes and then marched a further twelve miles, still westward, through winding roads and low hills to the small and scattered village of Bléquin.

After settling into their camp on the outskirts of the village, the soldiers were given leave to explore their surroundings.

'I'm heading straight for the pub,' announced Owen. 'Going to drink my horrors into oblivion.'

'There are no pubs here,' explained Mick, 'only *estaminets*. Same thing, if you ask me. A place for a beer and a joke.'

'I don't care what it's bloody well called, I'm heading there.' Owen was adamant as he lumbered out of the tent.

'How do you ask for a beer in French?' inquired Ted.

'*Une bière, s'il vous plaît,*' Mick replied. 'But I'm going to try one of these famous French wines. *Un vin rouge, s'il vous plaît.*'

They ordered their drinks and found a seat near a window.

'Ugh. This beer is warm.' Owen complained. 'What's wrong with the place that they don't serve it cold?'

The small inn was full of soldiers. A babble of voices and raucous laughter rang out in the smoky haze. Everyone was in high spirits. Plenty of good-looking girls mingled among the men, many sitting on soldiers' knees and making eyes at them. Some men found it a good opportunity to try out their halting French, and were surprised that some of the girls could speak a smattering of English.

'Bet the woman running this place is making pots of dough.'

'Bet the girls are too, either upstairs or out in the bushes,' Perky agreed.

It was quite late at night when Mick and his friends lurched and stumbled back to their camp.

They woke in the morning with sore heads.

'Next time, I'm going to look further afield,' said Mick. 'There's got to be more to a village than its pub.'

'Next time, I'm not going any-bloody-where,' grumbled Owen.

'You just take it easy for the day, put your feet up and perhaps the quiet of this place will help your jitters subside,' advised Mick.

'Fat chance,' Owen replied, 'when you can still hear the odd bomb exploding over the horizon.'

On the following day, after exercising their bodies and washing their clothes, the three friends made their way along the stream back to the village. They noticed flashes of copper beech in the woodlands and heard woodpeckers and orioles.

As they walked up what seemed to be the main road, the only road really, which was hedged with rambling tangles of blackberries, a skinny boy in tattered clothes, a peaked cap and big floppy ears approached them. He carried a large square basket with a cloth covering its contents. 'Buy bread?' he asked, lifting the cover to reveal rolls in several sizes and shapes.

Mick and his mates dug some change out of their pocket. 'How much?' they asked.

'*Trois centimes.*'

'Will threepence do? Got no centimes,' said Perky.

'Okay,' replied the boy, giving them each a long roll. 'This a baguette,' he said. 'Delish.'

'It is indeed. But t'would be better with some butter and jam,' said Ted with a grin.

'What's your name?' asked Mick.

'Jean-Marc Labrun. I ten,' he indicated with upheld fingers.

'Where do you live?' asked Ted, waving his hand in the general direction of the houses along the road.

'Come,' beckoned Jean-Marc and led them to an old white-fronted house with a board hanging from a pole out the front window on which was written *Boulangerie.*

'That's a bakery,' Mick translated.

'Show off,' Perky was quick on the uptake.

'I did a bit of French at school. Not sure how much I remember, though.'

At a well-scrubbed table near the front door, a French soldier sat in his grey-blue uniform matching the sky in colour, smoking a pipe and drinking coffee.

'*Mon frère*, Philippe.' Jean-Marc introduced his big brother, who greeted them with a '*Bonjour*'.

'Gooday, mate. On leave?'

'For a short time. You like some coffee?'

'Sounds good. Yes, please.'

Philippe sent Jean-Marc inside to inform his mother of the presence of visitors. '*Va dire à maman qu'on a du monde.* More coffee, please.'

Two women came out with floured aprons tied behind their backs. The older one in a long black dress repositioned a straggling piece of hair that had escaped her bun. Behind her followed a younger version, with long ringlets tied into a bunch so that they swung at her back.

She too wore black, a long skirt with a crisp white blouse. She carried the coffee pot.

'This is *Maman*, Inès Labrun, and my sister, Élise. We call her Ellie.' Philippe introduced the women.

'*Enchanté*,' said Mick, Ted and Perky in chorus. Resisting the urge to wolf whistle, the men politely added, 'Pleased to meet you too.'

'You speak English well, Philippe. Where did you learn it?' asked Mick.

'I go to Paris a lot, and learn it there.'

'And which battalion are you in?'

'The 3rd Tirailleurs regiment is fighting in Belgium near Ypres.'

'At Wipers, you mean. Us too. We've come from the area around Messines.'

'Ah yes, the big explosion. We heard it, like thunder. Blew up the hills and killed many Germans. Very clever.' Then in a sombre voice he added, 'The Germans killed our father. He died at Verdun at the beginning of this war.'

'Is that why your women are wearing black?'

'Here, many women have husbands, sons or lovers that died in the war. It seems to never end.'

'Our sympathies to your women.'

'*Merci*.'

'Ours are sitting at home knitting socks and hoping that we'll make it back,' said Perky.

The conversation moved into comparisons of army life.

'How's life in your neck of the woods?' Mick asked Philippe.

'Neck? I don't understand.'

'How's life in your army, then?'

'Much better since Marshal Petain became commander. When General Nivelle was the commander, our soldiers were not happy: too many killed at Aisne, not enough to eat, too long in the trenches, no time for rest like you have now.'

'Sounds bad,' commented Ted.

'Reckon I heard something about all that,' said Mick. 'Your soldiers demonstrated against Nivelle, didn't they? And refused to fight?'

'Half the army was involved, I heard,' added Ted.

'Straight out mutiny, I would have called it,' said Perky.

Philippe continued. 'When Marshal Petain became commander, things got better. He gave orders and made morale better. He granted our soldiers longer times to rest and more leave to go home. He gave us good food too. We are fighting again!'

'Thank goodness for that.' Mick gave a cheer.

When they had drunk their bitter coffee, Ellie sidled up to Mick and whispered in his ear, 'Come.' She led him out to the back of the house where an old apple tree flaunted ripe red fruit. An easy silence lay between them. Ellie's poor English precluded much conversation.

'*Un pommier*, an apple tree?' he asked, testing his French vocabulary.

'Apple tree,' echoed Ellie. '*Avez une pomme. Mangez.*' She picked an apple and offered it to him.

Mick took it apprehensively, remembering the Bible story of Eve and the apple. Juice ran down his face as he took a large bite of the crisp fruit.

Laughing, Ellie pointed over the back fence to an orchard. '*Beaucoup de pommiers.*'

'*Et beaucoup des poiriers*, by the looks,' replied Mick, eyeing off the pear trees.

Then she led him to the potato patch and, smiling, said, '*Pommes de terre.*'

Mick chuckled and said, 'I know that one.'

'*Vous êtes très agréable*,' she whispered.

Blushing, Mick replied, '*Et vous aussi. Très.*' He wondered whether Ellie said this to all the Australian soldiers she met. He hoped she wasn't a prostitute. 'See you tomorrow,' he said as he led her back to the table. '*Au revoir.*'

Over the next few weeks, Mick saw a lot of Ellie. When she was busy at the bakery, he watched her kneading the dough and shaping it into loaves. He scrubbed the pans as the hot bread was put on the shelf of the shop. He chopped the wood out the back, and piled it under a lean-to shelter. He and his mates helped some of the farmers with the harvest, stooked the hay into pyramids and threshed the wheat. The different exercise tested their muscles but kept them fit. They noticed that most of the farmers were women or older men and presumed that any able-bodied young men were away at war.

The six weeks passed quickly, with long and longer marches, football and cricket matches, band practice and concerts for the villagers, and lectures on how to avoid the dangers of the new mustard gas that the Germans had developed.

The day before the troops were due to march back into action again, Mick got out his letter from home detailing his daughter's birth and his father's death. As he read it again, he wondered how he could ever hope to cope with elation and devastation at the same time.

Late that night and despite the curfew, Mick left his tent to find a spot where he could release his feelings in private. Squatting against a fallen tree, he could see the flashes of continued warfare on the horizon and hear the muffled sounds of the big artillery doing its job. He put his head into his hands and sobbed quietly to himself. Sobbed that he was unable to take his wife and new daughter into his arms and caress their soft skin. Sobbed that he was unable to take his mother into his arms and share the grief for his lost father. He took the photo from his pocket and lit a match so as to see it, even if only briefly. He lit another couple of matches as he read again that paragraph of his letter, then he sobbed some more. He sobbed for the fact that he was thousands of miles away fighting in a useless bloody war. He shivered as an early frost bit through his clothes, and then sobbed some more as he mouthed a prayer to his God, 'What the hell are you doing to me? What have I done to deserve this? I'd have been better off staying at home facing shirkers' taunts than all this.' Eventually he sobbed himself out and went back to bed but couldn't get to sleep until nearly morning.

Later that day, they marched out of Bléquin to the tune of 'Pack up your troubles in your old kit bag, and smile, smile, smile…'

10

Early October 1917

Back at the front again, the 37th were in the reserve trenches preparing for an attack on Broodseinde Ridge. The men spent a day bringing in ammunition, grenades, wires, tools, water and food, over waterlogged ground. After fierce fighting on the next day, the 3rd Division achieved its objectives, overcoming several German-held pillboxes and taking over four hundred German prisoners. Mick and Perky were given the task of leading a group of prisoners back beyond the trenches: that was where they were heading anyway. They commandeered some of the German prisoners to help stretcher the injured soldiers.

The 37th then had another brief respite at Menin Gate at Ypres. The break, however, was short-lived. They were soon back in the field aiming to recapture another ridge beyond the small village of Passchendaele which had been in German hands for months. However, the start of the Allied advance was postponed because of the unseasonable weather.

On the first Thursday in October, light rain fell. On Friday it drizzled, and by Saturday constant showers had set in. Sunday saw the advent of bitter drenching squalls that chilled and soaked everyone as they huddled under their waterproof sheets waiting for the order to advance. Monday was dry, but on the following days torrential rains turned no-man's-land into a stinking quagmire. The mud was inescapable. It stuck on boots, on clothes, and on faces and eyelids. Cold, cloying and wet, it was almost impossible to walk through. Feet were sucked into it and boots got lost.

Each step required a superhuman effort. Travel was slow. Taking great care not to fall off the duckboards, the stretcher bearers worked in parties of eight to twelve. One bearer led the way carrying a white flag, hoping that the Germans would give it respect. The carrying was so back-breaking that only a short distance could be covered before it was necessary to swap positions at the poles.

'Did ya hear about the guy who was sucked in and when they got him out he'd lost his trousers in the mud?'

'Bit embarrassing, hey?'

'Nope, he was laughing as much as the rest of the onlookers.'

'Shut up, you lot,' screamed Owen. 'Have you seen the look on the face of a bloke as he's sucked into the mud? The more he struggles, the quicker he goes under and never comes up again. I tell you, it's worse than the pain of watching a dying man die.' By now Owen couldn't escape his terrors even for a few minutes. He was useless on the battlefield.

It was difficult for artillery to find a place where the big guns could be stable and not sink in the mud. When they were fired, the recoil forced them further into the quagmire. The accustomed barrage for the soldiers to advance under was sporadic at its best.

It wasn't only men that were sucked into the mud and drowned but also lumbering tanks and struggling horses. It seemed kinder to shoot a horse than to let it drown – the one time in this bloody war that Mick wished he had a gun with him.

It was far worse leaving a man to die that you couldn't reach across the quagmire. It left Mick and his mates feeling utterly helpless. An unbearable guilt set in and came back to haunt them each night.

'A man could go stark raving mad out here,' said Perky.

'And there are many who do,' added Mick. 'Shell shock. You can see it in their eyes and hear it in their garbled gabbling or blood-curdling yells at night.'

'Yeah, poor old Owen's a bit of a basket case in all that.' Ted felt sorry for the lad.

'They sent him off on a Blighty, didn't they?' asked Perky.

'And they'll send him home on the next available ship. He'll never be the same again,' Mick added. 'Even his mother won't recognise her darling boy.'

Muddy water sloshed around in the bottom of the trenches, making it impossible to keep boots dry. Feet responded to these conditions by swelling into spongy masses, toes lost all feeling, toenails turned black, and shrunken boots pinched and scraped heels. Soldiers were issued with whale oil to rub into their feet. It stank but it didn't really make a huge difference.

'If only I could get my feet dry!' thought Mick. 'Or apply some talcum powder and put some warm dry socks on. Walking's so difficult, not a hope in hell of making much progress. What's the use of a soldier who can't walk?'

Quite a lot of Mick and his mates' work consisted of piggy-backing men with trench foot along the duckboards to the nearest aid post.

Very little ground was taken by the advancing armies in these conditions. And what was gained was soon lost again. Thousands were killed or injured, for the Germans seemed to have an uncanny accuracy in their firepower. A horrendous price was paid in numbers fallen. The Allies withdrew and counted their losses.

At the end of it all, it was very obvious that Perky was no longer with them. His gift of the gab was missing. What had happened to him? Mick told the story that he'd heard how Perky had last been seen when roughly grabbed by a group of German soldiers and taken prisoner. But it wasn't without a fight, they said; his fists, his boots and his hard-hatted head flailed his captors. What chance did he have, especially as he had no weapon?

'Do you reckon he'll come back alive at the end of the war?' asked Ted.

11

Late October 1917

Weary and dispirited from the horrors of Passchendaele during which their battalion was reduced in number to less than half of its original strength, the men were sent to the familiar rest camp in the peaceful countryside outside Bléquin to regain their strength and morale.

'Anyone interested in coming in to Bléquin?' announced Ted to all and sundry.

'Sure am. Count me in,' said Mick, quietly excited at the prospect of seeing Ellie again.

It didn't take long for a large group of them to amble over there, though Mick would have liked to be walking faster.

He headed straight for the bakery, and found Ellie serving at the counter. 'Hey. Look who's back again,' he cried.

'*Plaisir de vous voir!*' Ellie rushed out and threw her arms around his neck.

'Great to see you again too.'

'No Perky?' inquired Ellie.

'I'm afraid my good friend was taken prisoner in the battle.' Mick was still smarting from his loss.

'*C'est si triste*, so sad,' Ellie sympathised.

'Are you busy?' asked Mick, not wanting to dwell on the matter.

'I find Jean-Marc. He look after buyers and I be with you. Sit down and have coffee while you wait.'

Mick hadn't even finished his coffee when Ellie joined him at the table out the front.

'Want to walk?' she asked.

'Sure thing.' Mick was keen to have Ellie to himself for a while. 'I've missed you such a lot.'

'Me too,' said Ellie as she tucked her arm into his and led him on a tour of the village, first along one road, then along the other.

'Your English has improved such a lot since I was here last,' commented Mick.

'I try a lot, with many handsome soldiers,' laughed Ellie.

'I hope it's only speaking that you practise,' winked Mick.

'What you mean?' Ellie wasn't too sure what Mick was implying.

'Oh, never mind,' said Mick, wishing he'd kept his big gob shut.

They walked until they came to a low stone wall at the far end of the village's main road.

Ellie took a bun and a bottle of water out of her pocket and broke the bun in two. 'I made this one,' she said.

'Mouth-wateringly good,' said Mick.

'Mouth-water? What's that?' Ellie asked.

'You know, tastes good, delicious. You make delicious sticky buns. By the way, where's Philippe nowadays?' asked Mick.

'Somewhere. They don't tell where our soldiers are. He come home again on, what do you call it, holiday from army?'

'It's called leave. No, we can't tell our family where we are either. I don't even know myself half the time. But the mail seems to find us wherever we are.' He reached into his pocket and drew a photograph from an envelope. 'Look, I've got something to show you. This is my brand-new daughter. Isn't she beautiful?'

'Yes, very beautiful. How old?'

'It's October now. She was born in April, so that makes her six months. But she was just born when this photo was taken.'

'What's her name?'

'April Rose.'

'That's nice. You lucky to have daughter. You see her when you go home?'

'I certainly will. Can't wait,' agreed Mick.

'And who is this woman that holds her?' Ellie wasn't really too keen on hearing the answer to that question.

'That is Maggie, my lovely wife,' said Mick.

'Oh, you not tell me you have wife,' pouted Ellie.

'Sorry about that.' Mick was apologetic. 'She lives with my mother now, since my father died recently.'

'They like to be together?' asked Ellie.

'They do. They keep each other company. And Maggie helps with the farm work as much as she can. She milks the cows in the morning and Mother milks them at night. And the other one feeds the baby.'

Mick and Ellie wandered slowly back home again as dusk settled on the village. As they passed the houses, lights revealed evening activities.

'Tomorrow is Sunday. I borrow two bicycles and we ride to the beach. *Ça va?*' Ellie suggested.

'That's a bloody long way, excuse the French,' exclaimed Mick.

'Three hours there and three hours back,' said Ellie. 'You can do that? We leave early. Bring trousers to swim.'

'It'll be too cold for swimming,' said Mick with a shiver.

'Cold frightens you?' challenged Ellie. 'I bring lunch.'

Early next morning, they set out with the sun and the wind in their faces along the rough track to the main road, which headed to the beach north of Boulogne-sur-Mer. It was easy riding once they hit the main road, a long straight road built by the Romans, passing through low rolling hills often covered with small woods and quaint villages. Ellie had packed a loaf of bread, some cheese, a couple of pears and a bottle of wine that they devoured as soon as they got there.

'I'm so hungry I could eat a horse,' said Mick, panting from the exertion of the ride.

'A horse?' questioned Ellie. 'You eat horses in Australia?'

'No, silly,' laughed Mick, 'it's just a saying.'

When they had finished the bread and cheese and half the wine, they stowed their bikes and the pears under a bush and ran down to the shore, where the waves gently splashed onto the beach.

'Will you swim?' asked Ellie.

'No way! I'm chicken,' retorted Mick.

'You not look like chicken,' said Ellie. '*Alors*, we walk on sand.'

So they wandered hand in hand along the white beach carrying their shoes, paddling in the shallows and watching fishing boats coming into the harbour on the tide. An hour passed quickly.

'I reckon it's time we went home again,' said Mick, 'else it'll be dark when we get there.'

'All right. Race you up sandhills,' challenged Ellie.

They ran off quickly, each vying for the lead. As they reached the grassy crest, Mick stumbled and rolled down the other side. Ellie joined him, and they tumbled together ending in each other's arms at the bottom.

Ellie drew Mick into a long embrace and a kiss. 'I like you,' she whispered. 'A lot.'

Mick was enjoying the experience, but pulled away suddenly when he thought better of it. 'Sorry,' he said.

'No,' said Ellie, 'you are right. I forget about wife.'

They brushed the sand off their arms and legs, found their bikes, drank the rest of the wine, ate the pears and set off home again. With the wind at their back blowing them along, they made good time.

'I see you again?' asked Ellie hopefully.

'Of course.'

Mick got back to the camp before dark.

During the next two weeks, Mick walked over to Bléquin on several occasions when he had a break from exercises, marching, lectures or band practice. While there, he made sure that he kept himself occupied doing odd jobs at the bakery or on neighbouring farms. There was always plenty to do, and he still got to spend time with Ellie, but at a distance, and always in the company of others. No more 'Any time is kissing time', as the song said. Pity about that! But he had to remain true to Maggie at home, however hard that was.

12

December 1917

Somewhere in France or Belgium

Dear Maggie,

It's been a long time since I had a chance to write. And it's been a long time between kisses. I didn't even get round to sending you greetings of the season. Sorry.

I hope you had a good Christmas with Mother and your family. I expect April Rose got lots of attention and little presents. She must be crawling by now and getting into all sorts of trouble. How does she get on with Smoky Joe? No scratches, I hope, if she grabs his whiskers or pulls his tail? Keep her cool when it's hot.

There was a break in the fighting for Christmas Day. All was quiet on the front line. Even here in the midst of this hell, they gave us a magnificent feast: pea soup to begin with, then turkey and roast beef, vegetables, gravy even, plum pud with custard, and a choice of beer or wine. Rich food like that we haven't had since last Christmas in England. Our poor old stomachs suffered, I can tell you.

We are back where we fought when we first came over here. Much of the town is now obliterated, but we had a white Christmas. Soft snow lay everywhere, but gosh it was cold.

Things have been a bit quieter these last few months. Guess it won't stay like that. Lots of digging of trenches and repairing of roads.

I've been missing you terribly. Regards to Mother and kisses for yourself and April Rose.

Yours sincerely,
Mick

13

March/April 1918

Suddenly orders came to go south. Dozens of battalions, thousands of soldiers were moving south. They travelled on trains and on the back of lorries packed in like matches in a box. The last few miles were on foot. The roads were pocked with holes and littered with debris.

It was spring again. Grass sprouted at the edge of roads, green shoots appeared from blackened tree stumps, red poppies flowered in the fields. Even birds could be heard again. Perhaps there was hope for healing the devastated landscape after all.

Mick had heard officers saying that the Germans had intensified fighting down near Villers-Bretonneux. That must be where we're heading now, he figured. Later he learnt that the reason for all this movement was what they called the German spring offensive.

Some weeks later, near the end of an April day when Australian battalions were fighting alongside French regiments at Bois l'Abbé, a small wood of sparse trees, and Mick was totally exhausted from all the carrying, he heard a plaintive cry coming from under a bush. At first he thought it was an owl, but what would an owl be doing on the battlefield? The '*Aidez moi, aidez moi, s'il vous plaît*' was so soft that he nearly missed it. The poor bugger must be bad, he thought as he and Ted, who had been deputised as a temporary stretcher bearer, hurried over to collect him. They found a French soldier with blood gushing from a neck wound staining his grey coat into a bloody mess.

'We're here to help.' Mick said. 'Let's get you onto this stretcher and get you to the aid post quickly.'

'*Mon dieu*, it's you, Mick Mack. I'm nearly gone. Please hurry.'

'Philippe,' exclaimed a surprised Mick. 'How strange to meet like this. We'll be as quick as we can but it might be a rough ride for you. Bullets and bombs are going off everywhere around here. Just hang on and we'll do our best to avoid them.' Turning to his partner, he said, 'You remember Philippe Labrun, don't you, Ted? We met him in Bléquin and ate his delicious bread.'

'And you were sweet on his sister, as I recall,' added Ted. 'We'll take special care of you then, Philippe.'

There was no answer. Philippe's pallor and breathing indicated that he was near death; he'd already lost too much blood.

'Stop a minute,' said Philippe, when they had moved a little way from the action. 'When I'm gone, Mick, please find my family. Tell them I love them dearly. And I died with honour. It would mean a lot to me.' His request came out in short sharp sentences, all that was possible between gasps for air.

'Sure thing, and I'll take your things to your mother. Does she still live at Bléquin? It's a long way off.'

'No,' he whispered. 'They moved to Amiens to be near to me. They live with Uncle Henri in Avenue de Grace, number 64.'

'This might have to wait until it's all over.'

'Any time is good. *Vous êtes un brave homme.* A good man, indeed. Now I die in peace.'

14

It was some time before Mick's battalion had a rest period again. The 37th had ten days off and were billeted in two huge barns at the small village of Allonville, only four miles from Amiens. The whole battalion in two barns was a bit of a squeeze, but it was bearable.

'I'll come with you,' said Ted. 'Easier job for two, though you might prefer to be alone, given how fond of Ellie you were.'

'It's okay, as long as you piss off and go and look at the scenery if necessary.'

They got permission for an overnight stay and left early one morning, hitching a ride with an army truck into Amiens. They quickly found Avenue de Grace but half the buildings were merely ruined shells and number 64 was a pile of rubble. All the people had fled. How the hell would he find the Labrun family now? They could be anywhere in the whole of France.

'What do you reckon, Ted? We can't give up now.'

'There's a couple of people wandering around over there. Perhaps they might know where they've gone.' Ted tried to be helpful.

'*Savez-vous ou est la famille Labrun?*' When asking an old man where the Labrun family might be now, Mick was brief, for being more than that was beyond his French ability.

'*Je pense qu'ils ont bougé à Vignacourt.*

'Gone to Vignacourt? *C'est loin?* How far's that?'

'*Dix kilometres, plus ou moins.*'

'About ten kilometres, he reckons,' explained Mick. 'How many miles is that? We'll have to bum another ride. Let's go.' Nodding to the old man, he added, '*Merci, monsieur.*'

After an uncomfortable ride on a farm cart, drawn by a scrawny and flea-bitten old mule along a badly rutted country road, they reached Vignacourt with its winding cobbled streets and once-white up-and-down houses.

'Isn't this the place where all the blokes come to get their photo taken?' asked Ted. 'Some amateur photographer has a fancy backdrop on their veranda. We could do that while we're here. Would you prefer your picture to be taken on a horse or a motorbike, or with a pretty girl?'

'Let's do what we came for first,' said Mick irritably. 'A bakery would be the place, I reckon. Keep your eyes open for the sign of bread.'

They wandered around for about an hour asking many people whether they knew Inès and Ellie and Jean-Marc. They inquired at several bakeries but had no success.

Then suddenly Ted pointed to a young boy carrying a bread basket down the street. 'Isn't that Jean-Marc?' he cried.

'It is indeed,' replied Mick excitedly.

'*Bonjour*, Monsieur Mick,' said Jean-Marc, recognising him at once.

'Hello, hello! *Comment allez vous?*' Mick ran towards the boy. '*Où est votre mère?*' he asked. 'Where's your mother?'

'Come, I show.' Jean-Marc led the men to a small cottage on the edge of the town with its unmistakable sign of *Boulangerie* hanging lop-sided from the front door.

'I'm afraid I bring bad news, Inès. *Mauvaises nouvelles*,' said Mick when he finally found Ellie's mother.

'*C'est Philippe, n'est-ce pas?* He died?'

'He did, and it was in peace. He was hit in the neck by a sniper's bullet. I stretchered him out. Before he died, he asked me to visit you. So here I am.'

'*Mon Dieu!*' cried Inès, digging deep into her pocket for a large handkerchief to mop up her tears. '*Mon cher garçon!* My dear boy. Much pain?'

'Not for long. It was quick, before we even got to the aid post.'

'And now he is…?'

'He was buried just behind the front lines where he fell, not far from Blangy-Tronville. A makeshift grave.'

'But they put up a cross with his name on it,' added Ted.

'He asked me to bring his things to you,' continued Mick. 'He thought you might take comfort from them.' Mick handed over Philippe's slim Bible and his pay book. 'And there were these photos that he had with him too.'

'*Merci beaucoup*. You are kind.'

'Can I be the one to let Ellie know, please.'

'She come soon. *Se vendant le pain*. She sell the bread in town.'

Five minutes later, Ellie turned up to find her mother in tears. A rush of empathy and fondness overtook Mick at the sight of her again.

'What happened?' she asked.

'Let's go for a walk and I'll tell you. Ted, you stay here and give Inès a cup of coffee.'

'I show you the wood,' said Ellie. 'It is pretty with bluebells.'

He held her hand as they walked to a copse of silver birch trees grounded with a blanket of wild bluebells giving off a sweet perfume.

'See, I tell you, pretty,' said Ellie. 'Now why does *Maman* cry?'

'Come and sit down first. Over here.' Mick gently shepherded her to a grassy spot and sat her down under an overhanging branch. He tried to break the news gently, pulling her into his arms as he did so.

'*Tenez-moi*. Hold me tight,' she begged and buried her head in his soft embrace while she cried and cried.

'Here, have my hanky,' said Mick, getting it out of his pocket. 'It's a clean one, so don't worry.'

He felt sorry for her, losing her beloved brother. It brought back to him Joe's death, which he hadn't thought about for a long time. He had never really grieved for him properly: no tears or wailing or gnashing of teeth. He wondered if Joe had died with peace and acceptance like Philippe did. Would he ever know?

He held Ellie close, and stroked her hair, as she muzzled her face into his. Gradually he too allowed his tears to flow, although he wasn't too sure whether they were for Joe or Philippe or Ellie. But it was a comfort to be held close in someone's arms, something he had missed for what seemed like ages.

Eventually they became quiet. Ellie lifted her tear-stained face to Mick seeking his lips. Her soft brown eyes said it all. Mick tucked her hair off her face and behind her ears.

'You are nice and warm,' she murmured. '*Je pense que je t'aime.* You good to me and good to my family. I give to you *un calin*, a cuddle.'

She pushed him down on to the grass so that he felt the soft skin of her body, and she caressed him in places where he hadn't been caressed for a long time. He returned her tender kisses and felt a stirring deep within. Surely just once wouldn't matter. Maggie would understand, wouldn't she? She needn't even know.

Later when the pair surfaced again, Mick said, 'Now let's go and get our photo taken at these famous photographers in your town. Do you know where they live? I'll get a copy for each of us for a keepsake.'

15

18 June 1918

'I've been in the field for over twelve months now,' thought Mick, as he huddled in the narrow trench. 'I must be nearly due for some extended leave in London, or even Paris. Now that would be good.' He'd always wanted to see the Eiffel Tower aspiring to the heavens and Notre Dame Cathedral symbolising the grandeur of paradise with its flying buttresses and vaulted ceilings. Several of his colleagues had spent a week or two in London earlier in the year but Mick had missed out.

The 37th Battalion was on the battlefield again, this time near Monument Wood, just west of Villers-Bretonneux, not far from where Philippe had died. The monument stood as a symbol of some long-forgotten battle. The wood had been reduced to a forest of stark trunks and sticks by months of constant bombardment. The Allies had begun to gain the ascendancy in this area of the war and morale was high.

Despite all that, Mick was fed up with the war. 'How much longer can it go on?' he thought. When he came to Europe he, like the rest of the world, thought it would all be over in a few months, but it was now nearly four years since the war had begun, and nearly two years since Mick had left home. So many soldiers, mostly young men in the prime of their lives, had been killed or injured, had been violently mowed down. What an utter waste, what a terrible crime! And not only their own soldiers but Germans too. 'So many of them are so young. They are people too with mothers and girlfriends, no different from me: just happened to be born on the wrong side of the border. On whose side did God think he was on?'

He'd begun to think of Maggie and April Rose again. In a quiet moment, he took out the photo of them once more. 'My daughter would have had a birthday by now and be running around. I wonder if she managed to blow out the candle on her cake by herself?' He tried to picture them all on the farm: April Rose on unsteady legs chasing the chooks, Maggie helping her feed the lambs, and Mother reading her a story on her knee. He kissed the photo before putting it back in his top pocket.

The night of 18 June was balmy and moonless. Heavy clouds scudded across the sky, threatening rain. The 37th Battalion in Monument Wood was without a hundred of its finest soldiers, who had been withdrawn for further training. Enemy planes with their distinctive black cross emblazoned on their wings buzzed around above them trying to ascertain Allied positions before darkness fell. The men were only just in place at the front line ready to go over the top when a fierce enemy barrage broke out. Sentries sent up a Very light and discovered some Germans attempting to cut through the barbed wire directly in front of a machine gun which immediately fired at them. Lewis gunners and riflemen joined in while others hurled grenades into no-man's-land.

Mick Mack and Dwight Richardson, an American who was working alongside Mick to see how the Aussies did things, were standing with their stretcher at the back of the trench waiting for the order to go. Suddenly an enemy grenade lobbed into the bottom of the wide trench. Mick was blasted right out of the trench, killing him instantly. It knocked Dwight's helmet off but otherwise he was unscathed, his crew cut still intact.

Next morning when the fierce battle had died down, his mates managed to retrieve Mick's body and bury it on the edge of Monument Wood. Dwight fashioned a cross with an attached circle onto which he carved the name Mick Mack.

'That's not his name at all,' exclaimed an exasperated Ted, trying to contain his tears. 'He was Arthur Michael McKayson.'

'Well, how was I supposed to darn well know?' Dwight was apologetic. He took up another ring of wood and started to carve again. Then he sketched his handiwork, and gave it to Ted to include in a letter to Mick's mother.

Epilogue

September 2001

Even before the September school holidays had started, the Hubble family boarded a Qantas jet and set off for France. April Rose was especially keen to go, despite her arthritic joints and high blood sugar. She'd never been to France before or seen where her father lay, although she had a photo supplied by the Commonwealth War Graves Commission of the white limestone tablet that marked his grave.

The family decided that their first port of call would be the city of Amiens, just a short way from Villers-Bretonneux. They spent a day wandering around Amiens Cathedral in the company of a tour guide who showed them small cameos of biblical scenes carved around the doorways.

'This is how medieval people learned their Bible stories for they couldn't read,' he explained, and introduced them to the line-up of saints beneath the rose stained-glass window. 'All of them were kings or queens, you can see by their crowns and staffs,' he said. 'The soaring ribbed and vaulted ceilings above the nave give the impression of the grandeur and beauty of God.' He pointed out that the stonework labyrinth on the floor of the nave showed that this was originally a pilgrims' church to which people travelled long distances along winding roads and rivers to do reparation for their sins. 'The little stone cherub, elbow on a skull and resting his weary head on his arm, is watching over this saint's tomb. It's tiring work for a little fellow.'

Some fearsome-looking gargoyles extended from the edge of the roof were only there for purely practical purposes, to allow overflow of water from the gutter.

Tim soon tired of looking at all that religious stuff, as he called it, and wandered outside to see the people of Amiens.

'Don't go away from the square,' warned his mother.

In the souvenir shop afterwards, they found a postcard showing banks of sandbags in the nave of the cathedral in 1918 put there to minimise any shocks that stray bombs might have on the ancient building.

'Did you know that during the war the French paid the Germans a ransom of a million francs not to bomb their precious cathedral?' Robert was ever the teacher. 'And much of the interior was used as a hospital for injured soldiers during World War I.'

The following day, they visited Villers-Bretonneux and saw the museum in the Victoria school built with the offerings of pennies and shillings of Victorian children in Australia. They paid their respects at the Australian War Memorial and finally set off down the country lane to Blangy-Tronville to find Great-grandpa's grave.

The cemetery was easy to find. A tall cross of remembrance indicated its location, just a small cemetery with about forty graves in it. It didn't take long to find the right grave.

'Look, here it is,' waved Tim. 'It says, "Private A.M. McKayson, 37th Bn, Australian Inf, Date 18th April 1918, aged 22".'

'And above it is the rising sun emblem of the Australian Army,' Robert added.

'The same as the badge that was on the upturned portion of his slouch hat.' Stephanie remembered the photograph of her great-grandfather from Grandma's trunk.

'The memorial line at the bottom could be chosen by the family,' said April Rose, reading the inscription, 'Our beloved'. 'The our covers us all from his wife and parents through to you his great-grandchildren, and your children and grandchildren beyond that.'

Each one in the family then paid their respects by placing something on the grave. Robert's offering was an Australian flag, Sandra's some dried gum leaves, Andrea's a candle, Tim's a red plastic poppy, while April Rose and Stephanie had both written messages in pretty envelopes.

A moment's silence followed, each lost in their own thoughts. The sounds of a bird chirping in the rapeseed crop nearby and a gentle breeze swishing in the trio of cypress trees seemed to complement the silence rather than break it. They could all hear April Rose's muted sobs that were escaping despite her best efforts to remain calm.

'A lot of the other graves have flowers in front of them,' said Andrea. 'It's a pity there are none in front of Great-grandpa's grave.'

'You wouldn't be able to see the writing if there was a plant in front of it,' said the ever practical Tim.

'We could do something about that,' said Robert. 'We might be able to buy something in the village and plant it there.'

April Rose was touched by the thought. 'That would be nice, dear. I'd like that. Something that will last longer than our little gifts, something red like his big heart that Mother always said he had.'

So they piled back into their hired van and made the short trip into Blangy-Tronville. A small village, it had no sign of anything resembling a nursery at all. So after filling his car with petrol at the *station d'essence*, Robert inquired where they might find a plant for sale.

'Try down the road and round the corner at the whitewashed house. Old Josette Labrun has a large and colourful garden with lots of pots. She might sell you one.' The owner was helpful.

It was, as he said, easy to find. The whole family stood at the front door as Robert banged the brass knocker, but there was no answer.

'Give her a minute to get here,' said Sandra. 'She might be frail and slow like Grandma.'

'She might be potting around in her garden like Grandma,' laughed April Rose. 'Let's look around and see.'

They found Josette round the back in a small potting shed, looking on her shelves for fertiliser pellets.

'Hello! Are you Josette?' asked Robert.

'I surely am,' the stooped grey-haired lady replied as she pushed her glasses back up onto her nose. 'And who are you and what do you want?' Her English was only slightly affected by her soft French accent.

'We're Australians, come to see a family member's grave. He fought in World War I, and he's buried in your local cemetery.'

'I know the one. It's one of many in this district.'

'But his grave has no flowers growing in front of it. The people in the village thought that you might be kind enough to sell us one. Oh, by the way, I'm Robert Hubble and this is my wife, my mother and my children, from Melbourne in Australia.'

'Pleased to meet you. What were you looking for? As you can see, I have a large number of flowers in pots. Do any of these take your fancy?'

'We are looking for something heart-red,' chipped in April Rose.

'How about something like a geranium?'

'That would be great. We have them at home too.' Stephanie wanted to get a word into this conversation. 'I like that white one with the purple streaks in the centre,' she pointed.

'That's a pelargonium, a close relation of the geranium,' Josette explained. 'Just as lovely, though.'

'A deep scarlet one would be ideal.' April Rose felt that ultimately it should be her choice. 'Red, the colour of the heart and of love and all.'

'How about this one?' Josette held up a terracotta pot with a small but bushy plant in it, covered with scarlet flowers.

'Ideal,' said Robert. 'We'll take it. How much would you like for it?'

Avoiding the question for the moment, Josette inquired, 'First of all, tell me about your Australian soldier.'

'His name was Arthur Michael McKayson. He died in 1918, but he never got to see his beautiful daughter, April Rose.' Robert put his arm round his mother. She hid her head on his chest, trying to stem the tears again.

'My father was also an Australian soldier. It happened, you know.' Josette paused as the family seemed to be taken aback by this news.

'My mother always said that he was buried in the Blangy-Tronville cemetery too, but I can't see his name there at all. I think she must have been mistaken. There are a lot of little war cemeteries dotted throughout the countryside round here. After the war, they moved most soldiers' bodies from their makeshift graves at the edge of the battlefield into these cemeteries.'

Josette continued, 'My father's name was Mick Mack. At least that's what my mother called him. I don't think she ever knew if that was his proper name, so Mick Mack it was.'

'Mick Mack!' the family all exclaimed together. 'That's our guy too.'

'What a coincidence,' Robert exclaimed.

'One in a million chance of him being the same guy,' added Sandra.

'See, I told you he had a bit on the side tucked away in France.' Stephanie was triumphant. 'There must have been something going on in the bushes somewhere.'

'Stephanie, how could you!' chided her mother.

'I had no idea at all of this other woman.' April Rose looked shocked and ignored Stephanie's remark. 'He never told my mother about it.'

'I bet he didn't,' Stephanie sniggered.

'I think it's cool,' said Tim.

'I think it's out of this world,' said Andrea.

'Well, I think it's just so wonderful,' said April Rose. 'That means you're my sister.' She moved forward to give Josette a warm hug with much back patting. 'I always wanted a little sister. And now I've got one. Incredible!'

'I think that all this deserves my help when you plant this little beauty.' Josette laughed enthusiastically. 'And by the way, there will be no charge!'

With April Rose in the front of the van holding the pot, and a shovel and watering can in the back, they all made their way back to the cemetery.

'This is my father's grave.' April Rose steered Josette to Mick's plot.

'A.M. McKayson. Arthur Michael McKayson.' Josette let the

sound of her words sink in. 'That sounds nothing like Mick Mack! No wonder I never knew this is my father's last resting place too.'

Robert dug the hole, April Rose and Josette together planted the geranium, Tim and his mother scooped the soil back into the hole and patted the soil down around the roots, Stephanie watered the plant, while Andrea sang 'Amazing Grace'.

Another minute's silence heralded by a whole host of birds singing in the rapeseed crop and the sun gliding out from behind a cloud.

'Well, that's a good job done, then,' said Robert.

'An excellent job,' Josette and April Rose agreed in one voice.

Josette, ever homely, invited the Hubbles to return to her place. 'And now you must come back home with me to celebrate with a cup of coffee or a glass of wine. We French produce excellent wines, you know. I have a soft Shiraz in my cellar that I've been saving up for something special. And you young ones are lucky that I made a new batch of lemonade this morning.'

Over wine and lemonade, Josette shared what little she knew about her mother's time with Mick Mack. 'My grandfather Gérard was killed at the beginning of the war, so my grandmother Inès had to take over the bakery business. And then Mother's older brother Philippe, my uncle, whom I never met either, was killed at about the same time as Mick Mack. My mother never married. She said no one could ever match Mick Mack, so we were all Labruns. My mother's little brother, Jean-Marc, did eventually marry and now has six grandchildren. He kept on the bakery business. In fact, he became a very skilled *pâtissier*.'

Inviting Josette to come to Australia and promising to keep in touch, the Hubble family said their goodbyes.

'And I'll look after our father's plant for the rest of my life so that he is not forgotten,' promised Josette as she waved them off.

Acknowledgements

This is a work of fiction. Some events in this story were inspired by historical incidents, but no character is intended to depict an actual person and all interaction between characters is fictional.

During my research, many books and illustrations were consulted to capture the atmosphere of World War I, but more specific to this story are the following: N.P. McNichol's *The Thirty Seventh: A History of the Thirty Seventh Battalion, AIF, World War 1*; Donald Munro's *Diaries of a Stretcher Bearer, 1916–1918*; the DVD narrated by Jack Thompson, *Winning World War I: The Western Front Diaries*; and an internet account of two brothers on the same boat as Mick Mack in A Family at War www.graemecheeseman.com/afamilyatwar.htm. The words of the song 'Boys of battle' are from http://acms.sl.nsw.gov.au/album/albumview.

Great thanks are due to Alex Junke of Tickera and Ray Tyndale for their expertise in French; to Ray Tyndale, Nicki Hunt, Helen Mitchell and Maureen and Fred Mitson, who commented on drafts of this work and for their encouragement and suggestions; and to Jim Breuer, who trekked around the battlefields of the Somme with me. Dr Richard Reed, the historian from the Australian War Memorial who accompanied us on our tour, was wondrously informative and filled his commentary with personal stories of the soldiers involved.

I have also appreciated the contribution of Stephen and Brenda Matthews of Ginninderra Press. And not to forget my writing group, North Eastern Writers, for listening to excerpts.

Without you all, this book would not have seen the light of day – it would have been buried alive in the bottom of my cupboard!

Finally, this story is dedicated to those in my wider family who fought in World War I. The Harper brothers, Joseph and Denis, and the Pickering brothers, Felton and Howard, fought for the Allies. Their cousin, Allan Pickering, was killed on the Somme. One of the Breuer brothers, Nicolaus or Jean, fought for the Germans, while Heinrich Breuer was interned at Holsworthy Concentration Camp in NSW for the duration of the war. May they, too, be 'Not forgotten'.